CLAN CASTLES 2: UPGRADE PACK

EVAN JACOBS

SADDLEBACK
EDUCATIONAL PUBLISHING

red rhino
b oo k s®

SADDLEBACK
EDUCATIONAL PUBLISHING
www.sdlback.com

Copyright ©2016 by Saddleback Educational Publishing

ISBN-13: 978-1-62250-977-5
ISBN-10: 1-62250-977-3
eBook: 978-1-63078-287-0

Printed in Malaysia

21 20 19 18 17   2 3 4 5 6

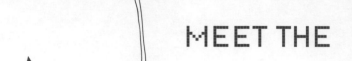

PRINCE ROBO

Age: 35

Family: an awesome older sister who rules a fierce castle

Secret Wish: to beat his brother and become king

Favorite Hobby: knitting

Best Quality: well-groomed

CHARACTERS

Erik Evans Syke

Age: 40

Favorite Food: ramen noodles

Biggest Secret: gets lost even with GPS

Pet Peeve: people who don't recycle

Best Quality: passionate about his work

1
A WIN?

Jake and Kyle were glad. They had won *Clan Castles*. Beaten Nojra. It felt good. Now it was time for breakfast. Their stomachs growled.

"What's that smell'?" Kyle asked.

Eggs! Bacon! Pancakes!

Bacon!

Eggs!

Pancakes!

"My parents made breakfast!" Jake smiled.

"Great. I'm starving," Kyle said.

"Winning *Clan Castles* will do that."

They walked out of the living room. The boys got closer to the kitchen. The smell was even better.

Looking into the kitchen, the boys' jaws dropped. Jake's parents had made a feast. There were plates of eggs. More plates with bacon and sausage. There were banana pancakes. Golden waffles. Even big pitchers of orange juice. Freshly squeezed!

"This is epic," Jake said.

"Your parents are the best."

Kyle and Jake grabbed two empty plates. They filled them with food. The boys poured two huge glasses of orange juice. They sat down and ate.

"I can't believe it. We didn't hear them making this," Kyle said. "It's a feast."

"Well," Jake said. "We were busy."

"I'll say."

The boys kept eating. Then Jake's parents came into the kitchen.

They looked odd. Their clothes were strange.

Jake's mom wore something frilly. Not like her at all. Her dress was big. Fluffy. His dad wore a brown shirt. But it wasn't a shirt at all. The arms were cut off. He wore tights. Weird! His dad wore a belt too. There was a *sworderang* tucked into it. A combo sword and boomerang.

Not Again!

3

A sworderang? Wait. What?

"Enjoying your feast?" Jake's mom asked.

"Yeah," Jake said slowly. "It's great."

"It was the least we could do. After what you boys did for the kingdom." His dad smiled.

"Ring the bell if you need anything," his mom said. She pointed to a bell. Then they left.

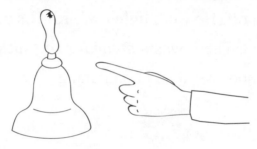

"Jake …" Kyle chewed a piece of bacon. "What's going on?"

"Well—" Jake began.

Boom! Boom!

Jake's house shook hard. It swayed. Back and forth. Back and forth. The boys took cover. Got under the table. Their food fell to the floor.

4

"What was that?" Kyle yelled.

"I think it's a quake," Jake said. He looked out from underneath the table.

"Quakes don't blow up! They shake," Kyle said.

Jake quickly got up. He walked out of the kitchen.

"Where are you going?" Kyle asked. He grabbed more bacon. Then followed after his best friend.

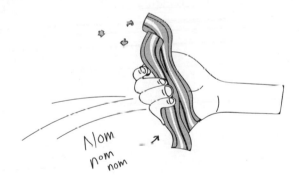

Nom nom nom

5

2
CLASH OF
WORLDS

Jake was standing on the front lawn. His mouth was open. He couldn't believe what he was seeing. Kyle ran up behind him. His mouth dropped open too.

There had been a big tree. It used to be in front of Jake's house. The boys played on it all the time.

Now? There was a hole. A big hole. It was bottomless. The tree was gone. Its roots were gone.

"It's over there," Jake said.

"What?" Kyle looked up. He saw the tree. It had crushed the house across the street.

Then they noticed the cars. They were overturned. Some were on fire.

"Jake ..." Kyle sounded scared. "I want to go back inside the game."

They both looked up. Angry skeletons circled above. There was a group of giant *minagons*. Half-minotaurs, half-dragons. They flew high above the skeletons. They were grabbing planes. Playing with them like toys.

Then a pack of *boarwolves* ran down the street. The half-boars, half-wolves were crazy. Snapping. Snarling. Snorting.

BOARWOLF

9

A *liongator* appeared. It seemed to leap at them. The half-lion, half-alligator was mean. It came from behind a house.

Had it been waiting for them? Jake didn't want to deal.

"Run!" Jake yelled.

Kyle and Jake took off. They ran fast.

A car screeched behind them. The liongator bit it! It ripped off a chunk. Part of the engine was missing. Then the car exploded.

Thankfully nobody was hurt. The passengers escaped.

The liongator was knocked down. It looked woozy.

"Yeah!" Jake pumped his fist.

"What are you happy about?" Kyle asked. "It's still after us."

"Head toward the park," Jake said.

A *spiderfly* swooped down. It was in front of them. The boys got low. They kept running. It kept on them. Kyle was picked up.

"Jake! It's got me!"

"Kyle!" yelled Jake.

Kyle!

In a second Jake was caught too.

The spiderfly took off. Up. Up. Up. It was focused on the boys. Not on what was ahead. The boys closed their eyes. They had seen the tree. The spiderfly had not!

Boom!

The spiderfly dropped them. They landed on the grass.

Jake quickly got to his feet. He helped Kyle.

"Ugh," Kyle said.

Jake had seen a small brick restroom. It was in the middle of the park. The restroom was gross. Nobody went inside. Had it ever been cleaned? Jake didn't think so. The park was 30 years old. That meant dirty sinks, toilets, floors. Ewww!

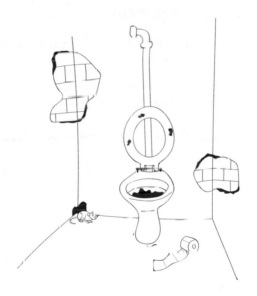

"We gotta get to that restroom!" Jake started to run.

"The bathroom?" Kyle limped after him.

13

Soon they were inside. Jake closed the door. Then the smells hit them. They both made a face.

"All right, Jake," Kyle said. "What's going on?"

Jake walked over to the window. He couldn't believe his eyes.

Giant-winged cats flew. There were flying snakes too. And they were really fast. Giant-winged rats ran on the ground.

"I think *Clan Castles* is real now," Jake said.

"How? That's impossible."

"Maybe so. But look outside."

Kyle stood next to Jake.

"Dude ..." Kyle could barely talk. "If the video game is in our world? If the serpents are in our world?"

"Then Nojra's here too," Jake said.

3
LET'S FIGHT

Jake turned. He headed for the door. "We have to fight him!"

"I agree," Kyle said.

"You do?" Jake couldn't believe it.

"I mean the army. Not us, dude."

Jake shook his head.

"They'll fight with guns. Bomb the whole city. We beat Nojra before. We can do it again." Jake opened the restroom door.

"How, Jake?" Kyle pushed the door closed. "Inside the game? We knew the rules. What levels we have to clear. What weapons we have. It's just us. Nojra. The serpents. We can't beat *all* of them."

"So we don't do anything?" Jake was upset. He knew they had to fight. "We know this game backward. Forward. Upside down. Nobody around here plays *Clan Castles* like we do. This is our big chance! We can show everyone. Gaming isn't a waste of time."

Hours of gaming was not a waste!

Kyle eyed Jake. He shook his head. "Fine, but if we die? I'm gonna kill you!"

They walked out of the restroom. Looked around. Then jumped for cover.

"Duck!"

A large fireball flew over their heads. It smashed into the ground.

The boys looked up. The blue sky was dark.

"Oh no," Jake said.

"What? Why did you say that? Jake?"

King Nojra floated in the sky. He was above them. Larger than ever. His tail whipped. Back. Forth. Back. Forth. Smoke came out of his nose. He smiled at the boys.

Then Nojra started to shape-shift. He got bigger. And bigger. Then he stopped. Something came out of him. An evil twin? No way. But it blew out smoke. It floated in the air. And it glared at the boys. The "twin" looked mad.

Wait, there are two of them?

Jake got to his feet. "Can't take us alone?"

"Don't piss him off," Kyle said.

"This time," Nojra yelled. "My twin brother can have some fun. He will see. Playing this game is great."

"Brother?" Kyle said. "Jake!"

"Oh! I read about him." Jake smiled. "Prince Robo! There was an upgrade. He was supposed to be in it. But then the company said no way. Told the game maker to stop."

"Too bad for you," Robo said. His voice was deep.

The evil king shot fireballs. So did his bad brother. Jake and Kyle dodged them. Kyle headed toward the restroom. Jake grabbed him.

"What are you doing? We need cover!"

"They'll destroy it," Jake said. "Follow me!"

The boys moved through trees. Then they ran. They were out in the open again.

4
HIDE!

"Go to the school!" Jake yelled.

He looked behind him. Kyle was still there. Jake looked at his school. It was the weekend. They usually stayed away from school. Why ruin a day off?

Today? Zero choice.

A large field was in front. There was a playground. Basketball court. Handball court. There were a few benches too.

Jake noticed something. It floated in the air. Caught the sun. "The Mirror of Reflection," he said. He rushed toward it.

The Mirror of Reflection

"It's too easy, Jake," Kyle said. "It's gotta be a trap."

"It's in the game, Kyle! *Clan Castles* has to follow its rules. Even here."

Boom!

The ground blew up. A sentry came through the dirt. He was big. Muscular. Much bigger than in the game. Sentries protected things. They were guards.

"He's the size of my house," Jake said.

The guard stood tall. The mirror was behind him.

He made a move. Ran for Jake and Kyle. The boys avoided him. The guard was too big. He tripped over his own feet. The ground shook as he fell.

"Let's get out of here!" Kyle grabbed Jake.

Jake eyed the mirror. He saw Nojra and Robo. They were coming.

Jake ran up the guard's large arm. Then leapt into the air. Flew over the guard's back. Then landed on the ground. There it was! The mirror!

Jake grabbed it. He turned toward his enemies.

26

"See you back in the game," Jake said.

Nojra and Robo shot out fireballs. The mirror blocked them. But the fireballs didn't bounce back. Instead, the mirror broke.

"What?" Jake couldn't believe it. "It doesn't work!"

"Jake!" Kyle yelled.

The giant guard was up. Back on his feet again. He had picked up Kyle. Kyle was dangling in the air!

"Kyle? Are you okay?"

"What do you think?"

Nojra and Robo laughed.

The guard spun Kyle. He was going to throw him.

Then something happened. A rock slammed into the guard's forehead. He slipped. Then fell. Hit the ground.

Jake looked up. He frowned. It was Avery

27

McQuade. She held a slingshot. Why was Avery here?

She was the reason the sentry went down. Jake and Avery had never been friends. They fought about everything. Sports. Gaming. Homework.

"You're welcome!" Avery grinned.

Avery
McQuade →

5
TEAMWORK

"Jake? Help me!" Kyle yelled.

Jake and Avery ran over to him. The sentry was out cold. Jake helped Kyle to his feet.

"Are you okay?" Jake asked.

"He's fine." Avery touched the sentry's nose. He didn't move.

Nojra and Robo laughed harder. "In this game? We have all the power!" Nojra said. "Rules don't matter!"

"There's nothing you can do. We can't be stopped!" Robo said.

They shot out more fireballs.

Jake, Kyle, and Avery ran. They followed Jake. He ran through the school. Fireballs hit some classrooms. The blacktop took hits too. So did the cafeteria.

"Well," Avery said. "We'll never eat there

again. Too bad. The food was so good. Ha-ha!"

"How can you joke?" Jake yelled.

"Yeah," Kyle said. "We're about to die!"

Avery rolled her eyes. "Follow me!" She ran ahead of Jake. She led them away from the school. And into her neighborhood. It was filled with big houses.

Jake looked up at the sky. "Where'd they go?" He couldn't see Nojra or Robo.

"Who cares? We're almost home." Avery ran faster. Jake and Kyle followed.

"Look, I played *Clan Castles* last night. Everything was fine." Avery stood in her living room.

Avery's home was large. Much larger than Jake's. It was two stories. In the living room was a large flat-screen TV. In front of it was Avery's PS4.

"Those explosions? Well, they woke me up. There was also a fire."

"Where's your mom?" Jake asked.

"Why?"

"My parents were acting weird today. Like characters in *Clan Castles*."

"I didn't see my mom. But she made me a big cake. She's always baking."

"Did she say why? What's the cake for?" Jake asked.

"No." Avery frowned. "But it had writing on it. 'Congratulations! The kingdom is free!' That's what she wrote."

"Oh no," Kyle said.

"I thought she was acting odd. She thinks the game is cool. I almost cleared Level 99. Told her about it. Thought the cake was about that."

"Look," Jake said. "Somehow the game is here. In the real world. Right now! At least you aren't acting weird. Well, no weirder usual."

"Very funny, loser," Avery said

"Hey!" Kyle got between them. "We've gotta call the police. See if there are any adults—"

"Adults don't play *Clan Castles*." Avery looked around the room. They would need weapons. "They won't be any help."

"If only I had a sworderang," Jake said.

"What would it matter?" Kyle asked. "There are no rules. Not in the real world. Nojra said that. He and Robo can blow everything to bits!"

"Dragons can't keep breathing fire," Avery said. "They have to hold on to it. Otherwise they won't be able to fly."

"I don't think dragon rules apply. At least not to Nojra and his brother."

"How do you guys know so much?" Avery stomped her foot.

Jake and Kyle told her everything. Told her about clearing Level 99. Told her how they were sucked into the game. Told her they beat Nojra from the inside.

"I used the Mirror of Reflection. Beat the

king in this own game." Jake looked smug.

Avery stared at them. "Yeah, sure you did."

"We did," Kyle said.

"Erik van Syke," Jake yelled.

Avery and Kyle looked at him. Was Jake crazy?

"He created *Clan Castles*. Lives around here," Jake said.

Erik van Syke's brain

Erik van Syke was smart. His brain worked like a kid's. That's why kids loved his games. But he was super old. Like 40.

He sold the game to GLive. GLive was big. Huge. The biggest gaming company ever. They bought the game. Wanted Erik van Syke to make changes. Take out characters everybody liked.

This made Van Syke mad. Very mad. He went into hiding. Said he would never work on *Clan Castles* again.

"Doesn't he live in a mansion? With gates?" Avery asked. "We'll never get inside."

"Look," Jake said. He moved toward the door. "We just beat Nojra in *Clan Castles*. How hard can getting into his house be?"

6
CODE RED

The kids rode Avery's bikes. They rode through the streets. Kyle was on one bike. He sat on the handlebars. He was guiding them to Van Syke's house. He found the address. It was online.

They were riding fast. Passing house after house. None of them could believe their eyes.

The real-life video game was crazy-scary.

Weird animals chased people through the streets.

Fireballs flew. Blew up. *Pow!*

But Nojra and Robo? They were nowhere to be seen.

Traffic stopped. Cars were left. Buildings caught fire. People tried to put the fires out. But they couldn't. There were too many!

The game was alive. Giant sentries smashed buses flat. People ran. Strange animals attacked them. Giant-winged cats. Skeletons. The creepy things laughed.

It was wrong. Who did this? It was epic.

"You know," Jake said. "I am crazy scared. But this version rocks!"

"Jake! I hate you," Kyle yelled.

"Only you would find this fun." Avery rolled her eyes.

40

Finally they found the Van Syke house. It stood high on a hill. Green grass grew on the hill. Large trees stood like guards. There was even a moat. A black gate kept people out.

"Oh, guys," Kyle said. "Are there stairs? This hill is steep."

"Stairs?" Avery asked. She was mad. "Do you see any stairs?"

"I was just asking."

"Come on, Kyle." Jake rode faster. "Where's your sense of fun? We're riding up that hill. Pedal power!"

"My favorite game tried to kill me. I am not excited. This is not fun. No way!"

The flying snakes were back. They hid behind trees. Then flew out.

Duckanhas came after the kids next. Funny! Cute ducky heads. Weird fish bodies. Super sharp teeth. If one touched you in the game? Instant death. In the real world? Who knew?

The kids rode faster. They made their way through the forest. Going uphill was hard. The weird ducks laughed. Then bit the bikes' tires.

Chomp! Chomp!

Pop! Pop!

The bikes wobbled. They wouldn't work with flat tires. The three kids went flying!

7
CHASE

Splash!

All three landed in the moat. The kids tried to get out. There were leeches! Bloodsuckers! They were covered with them.

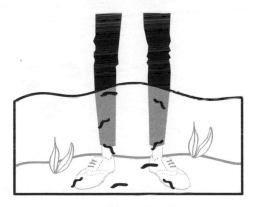

"Yuck! Oh my gosh! Gross!" Avery yelled.

"Ahhh!" Kyle yelled.

"Calm down!" Jake picked the worms off Kyle. They were on his arms. Neck. Head. Then Jake picked some off his own arm.

"Uh, guys?" Avery pulled at a worm. "We've still got a big problem."

They started running. Fast. The weird animals did not stop. The kids realized they were surrounded.

Avery got out her slingshot. She loaded it. Pulled back.

Avery's weapon →

The flying snakes' tongues flicked. In. Out. In. Out. The funny ducks showed their teeth. They moved closer. Closer. Closer.

"*Ah-woo! Ah-woo! Ah-woo!*" It was Avery. She was howling.

"What's she doing?" Kyle asked.

Jake shrugged his shoulders.

Soon they heard a crunching sound. It got louder and louder. They arrived in seconds. Coyotes. Real ones. The game's animals were surrounded. The creatures blinked. They had never seen the wild dogs before. They ran away.

"That was amazing!" Jake smiled at Avery. "How did you know what would happen?"

"I saw it on YouTube." Avery smiled. "I knew coyotes live around here. It's been on the news."

"You know what, Avery? You're not so bad after all," Jake said.

"Hm. Know what, Jake? You're not such

a jerk either." Avery patted Jake's shoulder.

"Uh, guys." Kyle's voice shook. He looked nervous. "Not to bother your lovefest. But what are we gonna do? Look!"

The kids looked at the wild dogs. Their mouths were open. Sharp fangs dripped with spit. Their gray hair stood straight up.

Jake, Kyle, and Avery ran. Van Syke's house was near. The coyotes were close on their heels. Then the kids came out of the forest.

Fireballs lit up the sky. More creatures

flew above them. The flying hairy rats ran around. Some were on the ground. Others were in the air. Strange wolves lurked. It was a crazy scene.

This was enough for the coyotes. They cried. Then ran off.

There was a tall black gate. Jake, Kyle, and Avery stood before it. Behind it was Erik van Syke's giant house. It was tall. And white. With pillars and columns.

"It looks like the White House," Kyle said.

Up close they could see colorful flowers. There were even small trees. They hadn't seen those from below.

The mansion was truly cool. There was chaos. But none of the creatures invaded its space.

"Well," said Jake. "This is where the creator of *Clan Castles* lives."

"Too bad there's no way of getting inside." Avery looked bummed.

And then the front door opened.

8
GAME MAKER

"I've been expecting you." Erik van Syke smiled. Walked over to them. He was typing on an iPad. But never looked at the screen. The man was wearing a purple robe. His long blond hair was in a ponytail. He even had a goatee.

"Shouldn't he have a butler?" Avery asked.

"Shhh," Jake said.

"Come over here." He waved to the kids. Van Syke took out a large key. It looked like it was from the game. He opened the gate. The kids walked inside. The gate closed behind them.

GAME KEY?

The weird animals continued flying around. They never got near the house.

"Well, well. I am honored. Three of my best players." He smiled.

"How do you know us?" Kyle asked.

"Dear boy, you defeated King Nojra. I created him. I created *Clan Castles*. I know everything about that game. Level 99. Amazing!"

He led them inside the house. They were in a large hall. At the center was a big computer. There were screens. Video game controllers. Keyboards. On the screen were numbers.

"I created *Clan Castles* on this machine. Those numbers? They tell me everyone who is playing. Or who has ever played."

The kids looked around some more. There were no pictures on the walls. No decorations. Nothing. What did this man do all day? Code. That's what he did. All day. Every day.

TVs circled the big computer. There were

about 10 of them. It was odd. The TVs were dusty. Old.

What year is this from?

"So," Erik van Syke said. He sat down in a large chair. He faced the big computer. "What brings you three here today?"

"Why are we here?" Avery was shocked. "Look outside! Your great game has gone nuts."

"Oh, that? Too bad." Van Syke started to type on his iPad again. "I thought you came to talk. How much do you love *Clan Castles*?

54

Want to know what's next? I thought you might want to find out."

The kids looked at each other. They didn't expect this.

"Nobody wants the game to be great. GLive wants cheap tricks. They want it to be easy. They want to make tons of cash. Sell my baby for the best price. Well, I won't let them."

Van Syke looked sad. He was yelling.

The kids were confused.

"That's why this is happening." Van Syke waved his arms. "I made this new game. It's the real deal," he said. "I want to destroy *Clan Castles!*"

"No! You can't. That's crazy!" Jake couldn't hold back. Van Syke was nuts.

"Is it? Look outside! Look at what I've made. I wanted to merge both games.

Every player should have the app now. I would load it through my computer. But it didn't happen that way. I was seconds from success. Then you two! Wow! I was stunned. You cleared the game. Then something went wrong."

Erik van Syke pointed at Jake and Kyle. Then he went back to his iPad.

"You two beat Nojra in the game! Level 99. The old and new games merged. When you came out? It came out with you."

The game maker stood. Walked away from them. He carried his iPad. Typed something. Then he quickly turned around.

"So call me crazy, if you like. I don't care. I don't care what happens to the game. I am happy. Because look at this …"

He pulled open some nearby drapes. They were dusty.

"The game will be banned. I hope. Then nobody will ever play GLive's version again. It will be dead."

"Look," Jake said. "You may not care anymore. But what about the world you're taking down? You have to live in it too. You're going to hurt people. And why? Just because a company took control of your video game?"

Van Syke looked at Jake. Had Jake's words gotten through?

"Ha-ha-ha. You're not coming here to thank me? To give me praise? After all, you love *Clan Castles*. You're just like everybody else. You want to complain. To tell me what I've done is wrong." Erik van Syke was upset now.

"We want you to help us," Kyle said. "Help us stop Nojra."

"I made many games before *Clan Castles*. And I will make many more. I don't need you! I don't need anyone! Get out."

Erik van Syke pointed at the door. "Out!" he said.

Jake, Kyle, and Avery walked out.

9
THE FINAL CLASH

"Great!" Kyle said. The kids walked toward the gate. "Now what?"

Nobody answered. Then Nojra and

Robo appeared. They flew through the sky. The evil twins seemed happy. None of the creatures had come past the gate. None had flown above the big house. Until now.

"He probably sent them here," Jake said. He felt bitter. Jake hid behind some trees. Kyle and Avery followed.

The fireballs started to fly again. The trees were too small. In seconds they were on fire.

Really getting old!

The kids ran. This was getting old. Fireballs blew up around them.

60

Nojra and Robo laughed. The kids could get blasted easily. But the evil ones were having fun. They were toying with Jake, Kyle, and Avery.

The three went to the open gate. Then jumped aside. A giant horse came through it. Of course it was not a normal horse. Whatever. They were used to crazy now.

"Ahhh!" The kids took off again. The horse chased after them.

Avery tripped. Jake and Kyle moved to help her. The horse reared up. It seemed ready to stomp on her.

Avery got out her slingshot. Loaded it with a small rock. She'd hidden it in her pocket. She pulled it back. Let it fly.

Whack!

The rock hit the horse on the head. It made a yelping noise. Then ran off.

The kids started to run again. Then Nojra appeared in front of them. They turned. Robo was behind them. They were trapped.

The creatures in the sky circled around

them. Sentries came through the gates. They marched toward them. The earth shook. The kids were trapped.

"Let's get rid of you three. Then nobody will be able to stop us," Nojra said. "Nobody will ever know you defeated me."

"Someone will know. Someone will beat you again," Jake yelled.

"Yeah! May not be us," Kyle said. "But you can't rule the world forever."

"You want us? Come get us!" Avery pulled back her slingshot. She looked fierce.

Nojra laughed.

Robo laughed.

The sentries laughed.

All the creatures laughed.

"We control everything," Nojra said. His voice was loud. Louder than it had ever been. "Now and forever!"

63

Then the king's eyes glowed.

Robo's did the same.

Two white beams shot from each eye. The beams joined. They formed one beam. It moved toward Jake, Kyle, and Avery.

Then Erik van Syke appeared.

 64

He was holding his iPad. He held it up high. It stopped the beam. The beam bounced back. Return to sender. Right in the eyes of the evil prince and king.

White light flashed. It seemed to cover the world.

"Cover your eyes!" Jake yelled.

He pulled Kyle and Avery to the ground.

There was a huge sound. Louder than anything they had ever heard. Louder than Nojra's voice. It seemed to echo. Bounce off the earth and sky.

It got louder.

And louder.

Until it was gone.

10
NEW GAME

A few minutes passed. The kids opened their eyes. They looked up.

The sky was blue. And clear. The weird animals were gone. Erik van Syke had his back to them. He held his iPad at his side. He stared down the hill.

"They're gone," Jake said.

"No way!" Kyle smiled. He pumped his fist.

"He did it," Avery said. "You saved us, Mr. Van Syke!"

Van Syke turned around. He was smiling.

"And you three saved me." He stared at

them. "I had become bitter. After I lost *Clan Castles*, I was mad. I forgot something. I love making video games. Coding is my life. I took out my anger on the game. I took it out on loyal players. Players like you. The ones who never give up. I make the games for you. I was wrong. I am sorry."

✓ Coding

```
var canvas = d3.select ("#" + initial.holder)
     .append("svg:svg")
        .attr("width", initial.wSvg)
```

"Where did they all go?" Jake looked around. He really wanted to know.

"Here." Van Syke held up his iPad. "It is *my* game after all. I sold it. And I thought I had lost it. No more talent. I thought my imagination was gone. You three showed me the way. Showed me it wasn't true. I didn't need to break *Clan Castles*. I didn't need to hurt the players. You know what?" He looked at the kids. "It's time for me to make new characters. Time for me to make another game!"

"So all those characters? They're in your iPad?" Kyle asked.

Van Syke nodded his head. Pressed a button. His screen lit up. It showed a new land. It was green. Filled with hills. In the center of it was a tall castle. Taller than any the kids had seen in *Clan Castles*.

Nojra. Robo. The serpents. The sentries. The flying snakes. And all the other creatures were there. Some were on the ground. Some were in the sky. The castle was tall. So tall it even went into outer space!

"I still own all the characters. The

animals from *Clan Castles* are mine. I've been coding a new game. I put them all in it." Erik van Syke was filled with joy. He held out his iPad to them. "And I want you three to be the first to play!"

NEW CHARACTERS!